DURANGO OUTLAWS

DURANGO OUTLAWS

FARON HANES

Contents

Prologue ... 1

Finding Fame & Fortune ... 3

Getting Down to Work ... 12

Tough Man ... 21

Farewell to Yuma ... 28

Convalescence ... 35

Onward ... 40

Hole-in-the-Wall ... 48

Pinkerton Detective Agency ... 56

Ten Men in Yuma ... 59

Gunslinger Jimmy ... 69

Rodeo in Yuma ... 75

Progress is Spelled Diago ... 79

The Next Adventure ... 84

Epilogue ... 91

About the Author ... 93

$\mathcal{P}$ROLOGUE

In the 1850's was when the electricity and telephone was built in Yuma Arizona. Street lights were in town only much later. Then electricity was installed in the homes and companies and stores.

By about 1902 the Sunset Telephone and Telegraph Company had set up shop. This Company, in 1911, became the Arizona Telephone / Telegraph Company and operated over the largest territory in the State. It was where Yuma and Durango City received telephone lines for their towns.

The first permanent entrance of the Bell system into the State was when the Tri-State Telephone Company moved in to Yuma, providing reliable and dependable service for the town. The Tri-State Company erected the line from El Paso to Yuma. It made it easier to communicate to the people of Yuma and long distance was available.

A flood of settlers followed these advances into a new city of the prosperous virgin land, known as Durango City. The advantages of the new telephone and electricity had made it possible to live a better life, but it was also vulnerability.

Along with Yuma and the casino on the Falling Rock reservation, Durango City was the prey of the biggest and the most notorious mob of the territory. These mobsters were trying to take control over the cities and the reservation, and had seized the opportunity of the people moving into the city who rushed to their get rich schemes.

The outlaws weren't too concerned about Yuma, as much as the casino and Durango City that was just starting out and could be infiltrated easily. Still, this was causing discontent with Yuma, which was caught in the middle of all of the take-over.

Never a dull moment for Durango moving from Yuma to the new town of Durango City. The mob was everywhere. The outlaws were causing havoc and needed to be taken out. Durango, with the help of his friends Eddie and Diago, was on a mission to shut them down.

Finding Fame & Fortune

Townsfolk couldn't help but notice the tall, dark and rough looking stranger as he rode into town. He was built hefty, and he looked intimidating, not only because of his size, but also the long scar on his left cheek.

He tied up his horse under a sign that read "Sheriff." As he walked into the jailhouse, he could see a man that was sitting behind a desk reading the paper, the Yuma Gazette.

Unfazed and casually looking up from his paper, Durango asked, "What can I do for you?"

"I'm looking to be a deputy in a small town and wondering if you have any openings?"

He put down his paper, and Durango responded, "What is your name?"

The man took off his hat, and his gray and black mixed hair showed that he had been around for quite a while. Settling down all would be a good move for him, thought Durango. "My name is Jericho. I've rode with the Texas Rangers and did some bounty hunting on my own to make some good money."

"The Rangers were all gunslingers and sharp-shooters," Durango said proudly. "My name's Durango. I did that too. I worked for the Texas Rangers. You must have worked for a different outfit? But you still worked for the Texas Rangers?"

Jericho gave a small nod.

Durango smiled, "That is a good reputation for the tough and a hardy bunch to work for. I want to see you shoot your guns. But if you're a good shot, I'd hire you on."

Seeing another man watching him from the corner, Jericho asked, "And your name is?"

"Samuel. I'm the deputy around here." Looking at Durango, he continued, "Can you shoot them guns, Jericho?"

"I sure can, Samuel."

"Are you fast at the draw in a multiple gun fight?"

Jericho only replied with a small grin.

Seeing the opportunity, Samuel continued, "Jericho, I've heard your name. You have a reputation as a good gunslinger. Durango is moving to Durango City in a few months, so we'll be needing a good sheriff for Yuma territory." Seeing he had Jericho's attention, he pressed on, "Jericho, how would you like to be sheriff of this here town? You both could share the duties as a sheriff until Durango moves to Durango City."

"Sheriff? I'd like that. Very much."

• • •

It was about lunch time and Jericho asked, "What do you say we continue this discussion over some food. Where is a good place to eat?"

Samuel said, "The Big Top Diner is the place where everybody in town likes to eat. It's just right across the jailhouse. The owner's name is Katie Joe and she is smart, bright and pretty. She is strictly business having to run the busiest bar and grill in the town of Yuma."

"Before we go, take a look at this." Durango hands Jericho a wanted poster from the top of the pile. "We have a man named Big Brawn that's on the run, broke out of prison and is headed some- where this way." Looking at the poster, he adds, "They all start looking the same, don't they?"

"Most of them are gunslingers."

"Let's go eat and talk more about your new posi- tion," says Durango.

• • •

As they walked across the street, Samuel was explaining to Jericho, "We got Jimmy going to start as junior deputy and Sindago along with him. We hired Jimmy and Sindago on when they turned 16 years old, to be lawmen. They still have to go to the Police Academy before they become full deputies." Seeing Jericho's confusion, he added, "It is like a boot camp for deputies. But they have each been shooting since they were 10 years old."

Samuel continued, "There will be more trained deputies, because of a growing town we need more law enforcement. But Jimmy and Sindago are both as experienced as six year deputies. They are natural fighters and fast at the draw. For now they will be working the casino on the reservation. There is always something going down in the casino."

• • •

As they walked in, the smell of the food was just so fresh and the scent of the spices and broiled onions cooking on the steaks just fills the air. "Pierre is the cook and he is a good one from France," said Durango.

Acknowledging her with a tip of his hat, Samuel smiled and said, "Katie Joe is going to get married to Durango. Did you know, he is lucky to be alive? It was an Indian, my wife's brother in fact, that took a shot at Durango from across the street and just about killed him. That would have been a sad day for Katie Joe. For us all. We had a peace treaty with Falling Rock Tribe, but that Indian named Bull shot at Durango. Bull, didn't want the peace, treaty but his father, Cuda, did. Now the peace treaty is still active because Bull deserved to die. Durango shot and killed Bull in self-defense."

Samuel continued, "I got a construction company called, Quicksilver and we are building another new bank and several other places in town. It's a good town Jericho. Its why I need a good sheriff, while I run my construction business. We like the town big as we can. That way when rustlers come into town we have other deputies, and a posse that can step in and shut them down. But I need lawmen with experience."

• • •

Samuel explained, "We have more champion gunslingers working under supervision, all reliable officers that are not bought off by the mob. Jimmy and Sindago are young but have the most experience of the 26 other officers of the law. But all the men each had to go through a tough and rigorous training of three months to become our deputies."

"You will need more deputies for here when we move on to Durango City," says Durango. "Samuel and his 100 men are working their tails off to get the town built as quick as they can."

"I'll bet," says Jericho.

Samuel said, "It will be an ongoing process between the electrical and the phone systems being put in, it's as busy as a hornet's nest, and as confusing too."

Durango added, "We got enough to contend with here in Yuma for now. With the electrical and the phone systems being put in, plus the town is getting a major store front on most of the businesses. Some robbers cut the lines and the power went out and so did the phones and a heavy load of money was stolen from the casino a few nights ago."

"They seemed like professionals, or just lucky, but they pulled it off," says Samuel.

"With the new technology that is available, the casino is just going to have to shut down earlier than 3:00 in the morning. They got away with a lot of money, they will have to close early that's all there is to it," sighed Durango.

Understanding the situation, Jericho acknowledges, "We will need trained gunslingers for deputies and others that can shoot like hell too. They need to go to the Police Academy before they become deputies. We got to keep up with the times, with the population increase and the many who robbed the place with the new rapid fire rifles that came into play, we need to be one step ahead of them."

Durango nods in agreement, "The thieves are becoming more hi-tech and we weren't ready for them, this time. For now we will be closing the doors at the casino at 12:00 AM and will have more deputies guarding the casino. The bank has a safe and only Frederick knows the combination. The money will be escorted to the bank by six trained lawmen and Jimmy and Sindago."

As their food is served, Samuel concludes their business. "What do you say? Jericho, you will have fifteen lawmen working around the clock depending how you schedule them. You will have lawmen that have worked for Yuma for many years and have been through officer training for three months. They just need somebody to be in charge which is you. Will you take charge starting tomorrow as the new sheriff, along with Durango temporarily till Durango City gets built?"

"I accept the offer."

• • •

As they wind down from their meal, Samuel notices Jericho looking around and says, "Yes. It's this busy all the time here in Big Top Diner. The food is delicious to enjoy. The price is right."

Samuel continues, "Get yourself cleaned up, and I'll take you to meet my wife, Shania, the Chief's daughter. We live on the farm just outside of town."

"So, where there was a good place to take a bath?"

"There is a pond about a quarter-mile out of town that people go out there and swim and take a bath, wash down their horses."

"Well I just might go out there today. I'm all dirty from weeks on the trail."

Overhearing the conversation, Katie Joe comes by to check on the men. "Well hello Katie Joe. Guess what? I'm finally stepping out of being a lawman, so I can run my construction company, Quicksilver, full time. This town needs a major overhaul. This here is Jericho, our new sheriff."

Katie Joe said, "I wondered when you were going to step down to run that construction company." Turning to the newcomer, she says, "Well it is nice meeting you Jericho. I am planning on going swimming down at the pond after the lunch rush. I would be happy to show where it is at.”

• • •

Meanwhile, Durango was thinking back a few years earlier when he and Katie Joe were growing up in Yuma. The “good old days” with Eddie and Betty Lou.

Young Durango had asked if Katie Joe wanted to have some fun. After some hot romance down at the pond, he asked her if she would want to go out for the evening for dinner. As she smiled “yes,” she said, “the Eatery at 6:00 tonight.”

At the diner Durango remember something he had told her earlier, and asked, “do you still wanted a diner of your own?”

“Yes, but I have no money to buy a diner.”

Durango said. “I will loan you the money for the diner.”

“That would be a wonderful blessing from God.”

They talked into the night about putting the diner together, and how awesome that would be. “See dreams do come true Katie Joe,” smiled Durango.

• • •

Snapping out of his daydream, Durango saw Jericho getting up to leave, and heard Samuel saying, “Well, I’ll make arrangements in the saloon so you can in one of their rooms until you get oriented. In the meantime, keep an eye out. Today is payday for the ranchers and they're going to want to come into town and celebrate."

Jericho said, "I can handle them when they get rowdy, I am not worried about that. If there is big trouble, Samuel, just give two shots, in the air and I'll be here to help."

And with that, Jericho got ready to head down to the pond to take a bath and wash down his horse.

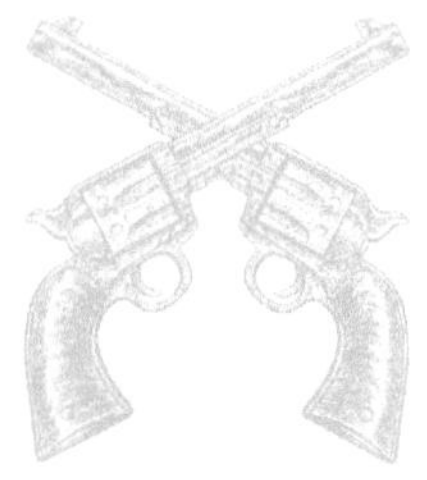

ᘍetting ᗞown to ᘺork

Durango headed back inside the jailhouse, and Samuel on foot toward the saloon to make arrangements for Jericho. Just as Jericho was untying his horse, shots rang out from the Eatery saloon at the other end of town. Jericho was first on his horse with Samuel following right behind, and other folks looking to see what is going on at the saloon.

It was a rustler that got paid early and was there shooting up the place. Jericho quickly got off his horse, walked in and said, "Put the gun away or I'll shoot you." The rustler pointed his gun at Jericho, but before he could even think about shooting, Jericho shot him in his shooting arm. The rustler dropped his gun just as Durango and Samuel ran in.

After a quick stop to see the doctor, one of the deputies quickly took the rustler out to the jailhouse. Jericho hadn't even unpacked his horse before making his first arrest!

• • •

His second action would come later that day. The afternoon stagecoach rode into town and the driver yelled, "We've been robbed of the banks money for the construction company. Just now, just outside of town! At least four of them!"

Well Samuel shot twice in the air calling out for Durango, Jericho and the deputies and construction crew to get together and chase them outlaws down the trail. A couple miles from town, seeing the large posse already on their trail, the robbers hid behind some rocks near the road. But one of them shot way too early, and the lawmen knew they were headed into an ambush.

Cover blown, the rustlers split up and tried to run for it. Jericho pulled out his rifle and shot the man that had the money.

Durango said, "Good shooting. We just got to get the other three." The other deputies surrounded the outlaws. Although one of the deputies got shot in the leg, he shot back and killed the robber. The others turned themselves in.

The corner of Durango's lip went up as he looked at Jericho, but said to Samuel, "Looks like he does know how to shoot after all."

• • •

Jericho was a handsome but a rough looking man. He was rather intimidating man, because of his size, and he could be ruthless. But really he was a friendly fella. He had seen a lot in his time, but he still liked to strike up conversations with the townspeople and tried to get to know as many people as possible.

He loved to whittle on a piece of wood. His specialty was guns and horses. Chatting one evening in the saloon, he said, "There is nothing like a sharp knife. Got to have a sharp knife when you're whittling." After he is done he puts them in his collection. Must have over 50 whittling jobs that he has done in the past.

• • •

A couple of days later, Samuel, rode up to Jericho who was sitting on the jailhouse porch and said, "Jericho, time that the rustlers will be pulling into town. I thought I'd be here to give you a helping hand." As he dismounted he said, "Sometimes they can get pretty riled up and start bar fights. Nothing very serious but still fight is a fight.

"Meantime, I'm going to go down to the store and check on Shania, and tell her that I love her and looking forward to having some fun tonight." He tied off his horse and started to walk down the street to see his pretty wife.

Just then, a man flew out of the saloon bar window and another rustler jumped out of the window for a fight. As Samuel watched, Jericho flew down the street to the Eatery and pulled the two apart and said, "If you don't settle down you are going to spend the night in jail sleeping it off." The two men, understanding his tone, shook hands and went back in the bar for some more drinks.

They paid for the window too.

Jericho turned back to Samuel and said, "Yes, it's about that time of night that the rustlers wanted to drink and fight." With that, Jericho went into the bar to keep an eye on things. That way there'd be somebody there to stop the fight before it even started. He sat in the corner of the bar at a table, ordered a beer and continued whittling himself a grizzly bear.

• • •

Seeing him eyeing him up, a cowboy walked over to Jericho and said, "that's a really, nice grizzly bear you got there."

"Thank you, I just do it for a hobby. Something to keep me busy while I'm keeping an eye on the bar and making sure that there is no trouble."

"We're just having fun, we mean no harm... just having a few drinks from a hard, week. So are you the new sheriff in town?"

"Yes, I am. My name is Jericho. Durango is moving on to another town soon, so I'll be the Sheriff of Yuma."

"My name is Boston. I'm going to own my own city some day in Massachusetts. I got the money to get it started and I'm leaving tomorrow."

Jericho wished him good luck.

"Yeah well everybody's heading out west. I'm going to move out east and start me a city. The west is just too wild for me. I was going to start a town out here in the west but I decided to move back east. I'm going to name the town Boston." And he added, "Maybe they will name the state Massachusetts. That is my last name, Massachusetts."

Jericho said, "That's some big dreams you have there. Good luck to you Boston."

"Yes, I have some big dreams. When my grandfather died he left enough money to buy me a state here in the territory. He was a very rich man. And he had nobody in the family to give the money to accept to me. I inherited all of his money and the property that I'm going to build a town called Boston. There is already people moving into Boston already as we speak. The land is rich, perfect for farming, raising cattle, and having an ocean waterway right next to the city."

"There will be a need for all of the lumber that will be sent down the waterways to the town where there will be trains to take the lumber west. That is where the town of Boston will be."

"And I'm going to build a shipyard for the waterways for supplies and merchandise to be shipped into Boston. Then I'll have the railways taking the merchandise to different parts of the territory."

Jericho said, "Well it sounds like a good plan. If you can pull it off, you'll be a very rich man."

"I saw the way you handle those trouble-makers. You know you'd make a good sheriff in Boston."

"I like it here Boston. I like the west. But thanks anyway," says Jericho.

"There are going to be lots of pretty women in Boston. A lot of brothels. I'll even pay you to stay in one and pay for your food, plus a salary. It is a good sheriff that the town of Boston needs like you Jericho."

"Well tell you what. I'll think about it Boston. I'll give you an answer in the morning," Said Jericho.

Good man, thought Boston. He liked whittling on bears too.

• • •

As he did every few days, Jimmy was heading out to the stable to groom Blazer for Durango. But today was different—a girl about his age was already there, brushing down and feeding a horse he didn't recognize. It was the first time they crossed paths in Yuma, and Jimmy was immediately taken by her. She was pretty and she was in fine shape.

While he stood there smiling and staring, she turned to look at Jimmy. As politely as he could, he asked her name. She said, "My name is Mary Joe. What is your name?"

"My name is Jimmy, ma'am. Is that your pretty Arabian horse?"

"I'm hardly a ma'am. But, yes, she's an Appaloosa.

She is strong and can run like a wild cougar. I had her since she was born."

"She sure looks in good shape. Do you like to run her?"

Mary Joe nodded. Jimmy was taken in by her smile and her sexy body. He asked her, "Would you like to go horseback riding someday with me?"

"Sure" she said, "That would be topper. Maybe we will see who is faster?"

"Yes, we will have to see, won't we? This horse I am grooming is Durango's horse. He is the sheriff of this here town." This didn't impress her as much as he expected, but he pressed on, "Are you going to go to the school today, Mary Joe?"

"My Pa's a farmer. We just moved into town. But when we get settled in, I'd like to be going to school."

"We can talk about setting up a horse race between us and others in town. We are having a town carnival soon, maybe we can have the race then?"

"Maybe so. Well, I got to go and help moving into our home right now, but I will see you later."

"Why not tonight, we can go to the Big Top Diner. I'm buying," says Jimmy.

"That sounds grand."

"I will meet you there about six-o'clock."

She said "That would be fine."

Jimmy had a big smile on his face for the rest of the day.

• • •

Later that day, Durango met up with Jimmy to take him out to shoot bottles, in exchange for Jimmy grooming his horse. "You feeling alright today Jimmy?" Durango asked.

"I just met a girl my age and we are going out tonight at the Big Top Diner for supper."

"That is how Katie Joe and me started out, going out to eat. One thing led to another, now we are married. What is her name?"

"Her name is Mary Joe, she is pretty and sexy."

"Well, I'll see if we are going to get along real good tonight at supper." Trying to bring his young protégé's mind back, he said, "Do you know that you are going to be one of my best deputies, the way you can shoot, and the way you handle your job without being intimidated? That is a good sign of a dependable, reliable lawman. I bet you'll be an excellent gunslinger; you're getting better the more we practice," smiled Durango.

• • •

Back at the Jailhouse, Durango was greeting his good friend, who had just ridden back into town after a few weeks away on a job. "Well, it is good to see you Fast Eddie. How are you and Dixie getting along together? I heard she had the hots for you," Durango grinned, adding, "And you had the hots for her. You old dog."

"It's good to see you, Durango." They shook hands and stared at each other with a grin on their faces.

"We both know how to shoot our guns and never back down from multiple gunfights. We were just talking about you, Eddie, and about how I need a good deputy in Durango City. Any chance that you want to be my deputy in Durango City?"

Eddie said, "That would be topper. We'd make the best lawmen around."

"Glad to hear it. We'll be starting as the lawmen in three weeks in Durango City. We are going to have us a new jailhouse and you'll have your own desk. Everything in Durango City is going to be brand-new. We are even going to have a new Big Top Diner right across the street of the jailhouse."

"The new bank in town will be called Keystone bank. And it will be right across from the jailhouse. So hopefully that will decrease the bank robberies. Because there will be a lot of money at the bank. It's the only one that's built so far."

"Eventually there will be two banks in the city. The one that will be handling the shipping and handling of the ships arriving by boat will be a different bank. But cargo will be transferred to the train station money and will be located at the end of town near the river."

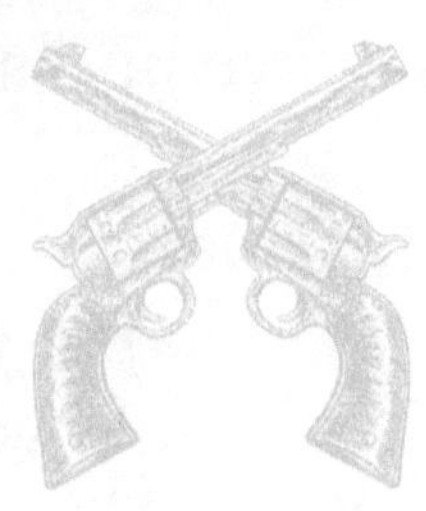

ᎢOUGH ᎷAN

The next day Jericho and Boston were having breakfast at the Big Top Diner. Jericho was telling him about his discussion with Job, the town's preacher. "I'm a gunslinger," said Jericho. "But then Jesus forgave me of this job. I don't like to kill. It is something I have to do for my job. I do it in self-defense. I do it to keep the peace around here. Job understands, and he knows we need a good Sheriff and Deputies to keep this town in order." And he added, "I love to teach people how to shoot a gun or a rifle."

"You could start a shooting school in your spare time."

"That would be a good road to take. Most everyone needs to know how to handle a firearm, what with the west being so wild." And then he quickly added, "I got a good idea. Why don't we have a tough man contest?"

But before he could get an answer out of Boston, Katie Joe walked up to the men sitting at the table by the window and asked them if they liked their meals? Jericho responded joyfully, "It was topper. One of the best meals I've had since I've been here in the west."

He looked over to Boston who chimed in, "I enjoyed it immensely, thank you." Boston then asked Katie Joe, "What would you think of a tough man contest here in Yuma?"

"I think it would be a good idea. We haven't had one in a while. Do you know Matt?" Boston frowned, but Jericho shakes his head. "A guy who likes tough man contests and would probably want to participate. And you too Jericho. I think that you would do very well in the contest, too. Three-way, five-dollar entry, winner takes all. I think people should know how to fight with their fists instead of their guns."

Boston said, "I'm not a betting man, but I'll bet on Jericho to win"

"Yes, Jericho is a pretty big man. He would do well against Matt."

Jericho said, "Let me get this straight. It is five dollars entry fee and the winner wins 15 dollars? I'm in. Let's see if Matt would pay the five dollars entry fee."

"Matt is just sitting a few tables away, so I'll go ask him." Katie Joe walks down the row of tables with Jericho and Boston watching, and says to Matt, "How are you doing? Are you enjoying your meal?"

He says, "It was just perfect. I'm enjoying it just fine thank you. How are you doing, Katie Joe?"

"I am as fit as a fiddle. Say, I was talking to Jericho, the new sheriff, and he thinks that we should have a tough man contest and wanted to know if you would enter? It would be five dollars entry fee and $15 for first prize? Would you be interested?"

Looking around to see the men watching him, he says, "Sounds fun to me, Katie Joe. I'll pay the five dollars. When is it going to be? On Saturday?"

Katie Joe replied, "Yes, Saturday at 3 o'clock. We just need a third."

• • •

Just then a lone cowboy walked in and straight up to the bar asked for a whiskey and beer. Sylvester the barkeep brought him over his drinks and the man said, "Put it on my tab."

Sylvester said, "We don't run tabs here. Cash up front."

The man gruffly questioned, "Isn't my word good enough?"

"What's your name, stranger?"

"Buck."

"Well, Buck, manager says it is cash only."

The man threw the money on the bar.

Jericho was keeping an eye on him. He seemed like he had an attitude and wasn't a very nice guy. Jericho walked over and invited him over to join him, but he refused. "We're having a tough man contest on Saturday. Seems like you might be the right type. Maybe you'd like to join in?"

"There is money to be made in it?"

"It is five dollars in and a $15 prize for the winner."

He said. "Sounds like my kind of fun. Who do I pay the five dollars to?"

Nodding toward her across the room, Jericho said, "Katie Joe can take the money. It will start around 3 o'clock in the afternoon on Saturday."

• • •

Soon enough, it was 3 o'clock Saturday and along with the three men, the townspeople showed up for the contest. "Who wants to start?" asked Katie Joe. Matt says he would, and Buck, the new guy name stepped up as well. Matt and Buck stepped into the middle of the ring drawn in the dirt of the street, and the fight was on.

They were two big men and they started out the fight wrestling. Matt hit Buck in the face and the fight really got going. Buck kicked Matt in the groin, then Matt returned with a hair pulling and the punch in the face. Buck threw Matt down to the ground and kicked him in the chest. Matt rolled over got back on his feet and put Buck in a headlock.

Buck stomped Matt on the foot releasing the headlock. The two were getting mad at each other as the fight went on. Matt hit Buck in the face about three times and Buck went flying back. Buck got up from the ground and wrestled Matt to the ground. Rolling in the dirt, they were both hitting and gouging each other in the face and in the eyes.

Then they both got up off the ground and Buck kicked Matt in the chest and Matt flew back falling to the ground. With that, Matt conceded, "Okay Buck you won the fight."

Now it was time for Jericho to fight Buck. Jericho was a big man and took Buck and threw them around like he was a ragdoll. Jericho quickly overpowered him with his size and his strength.

Looking on, Buck knew he had lost. He could stand no chance against Jericho. He was just too big. Jericho won the prize money! Showing there were no hard feelings, Jericho said, "The food and drinks are on me at the Big Top Diner!"

Katie Joe said, "We, got to have these tough man contests more often," as she smiled at Jericho.

He was the man of the hour. His money paid for the drinks from the contest. As everyone ambled down the street, Jericho didn't stop into the Big Top Diner. Noticing he had disappeared after the wrestling match, everyone was asking, "Where is the winner of the contest?"

Seeing the crowd and guessing the winner, Durango asked, "Where is Jericho anyways?"

Katie Joe filled him in, "He's down the street at the Eatery becoming good friends with Star. Guess he likes them pretty, rich women."

"Well that's good at least somebody's there to keep an eye on the Eatery."

• • •

Durango go back to his discussion with Samuel. The railroad had made plans for the railroad track to go through the town of Yuma. But the railroad's plan was causing trouble because the settlers didn't want to sell their land. And it seemed the railroad was sending in troublemakers who were trying to make them sell.

• • •

Down at the Eatery Saloon, Jericho was asking Star if she would ever want to settle down? She said, "With the right man you bet I would."

Star continued, "But it just seems that all the men just love to drink and don't seem to care about the woman they are married to."

"Star, I'd make a good husband."

"Jericho, you're a lawman and a gunslinger? Couldn't live wondering if you are going to die that day or not. You seem like the marrying kind to me Jericho. But because you are a lawman, I just couldn't marry you."

Just then Doc Holliday walked into the Eatery. Jericho stopped talking to Star and looked the newcomer over really well. Jericho wasn't sure if there was a wanted poster for Doc, but before he went to check, he waited to see what would happen. He didn't want to leave if he was there to start trouble. But he only sat at the bar and ordered a drink.

So, Jericho slipped out and went down the street to the jailhouse to check him out. He checked out fine. No posters on him for now.

Seeing Samuel, Jericho told him who he saw, adding, "Thought there was going to be some action. I'm going back over to the Eatery and talk to Star and keep an eye on things. It is that time of night when the rustlers come in anyhow. I'll be there to keep things in order." With a smile, he added, "It gives me a chance to get to know Star better, too."

ꟻarewell to Yuma

There was a big celebration for Durango before his move to be sheriff at Durango City. They even made a statue of him and put it in front of the entrance to the Durango Park. The celebration for the sheriff lasted all weekend long. There was a parade with Durango and Katie Joe as the hosts with all of the twenty-five deputies and Jimmy and Sindago riding next to the new Sheriff of Durango City. Even Fast Eddie was in the parade and the townspeople were throwing rice for the sheriff and Katie Joe. Music was playing and people were singing. It was a wonderful time for the whole town.

With joy from his heart," exclaimed Matt, one of the deputies, "We will all be moving on to Durango City someday!"

The rag top music and the dancing will go on all weekend long. There will be laughter and singing and fried chicken and beans that will be there for the ones that are hungry that night.

• • •

But they hadn't left yet, and there was still work to do. The next day it was Durango and Jimmy that pulled the morning shift. "That sure was fun last night wasn't it Durango?"

Durango smiled, "Jimmy, I think it was topper."

"Saw you kissing Katie Joe... and Samuel and Shania, too," the boy said with a grin. "I think I'll go visit them today. Well, visit Sindago. We're good friends, you know."

Durango stepped outside for a cigarette. As he looked across the street, it wasn't the lady on a horse he noticed, but the snake by the horse front legs. He knew there was going to be trouble.

Sure enough, the woman that was riding the horse got bucked off the saddle as the horse went frantic after being startled by the snake. The lady fell to the ground and the horses began to buck. Durango ran over and calmed the horse that was bucking wildly.

The lady was screaming out of fright because now the snake was by her. Durango took out his pistol and shot the snake dead. He went to see if the lady was alright, and she was fine except for being shook up.

"That was a close call," she said. "Thank you, Durango."

"You were lucky I was here, that was a rattle snake."

She said, "I just pulled in for breakfast at the Big Top Diner and do some shopping. I wasn't expecting the snake."

Durango said, "Let me help you up. Are you going to be alright? Your horse will be fine. He will be calmed down by the time you have, finished with breakfast."

As she walked into the diner, Jimmy approached Durango and asked, "Is that the lady in the church that couldn't walk, and Job healed her?"

Durango replied, "I think you're right."

"But, look at her now. She can walk just fine. Thanks to God and Job."

• • •

Most of the lawmen were at the jailhouse just talking amongst each other. Durango told Jimmy and the rest of the group that he was going to miss this place, but new opportunities await for him in Durango City. Durango said to Jimmy, "I got two more weeks here in Yuma. Then Fast Eddie and me will be sheriff and deputy in Durango City."

"Bronson wants to be a Lawman. He's giving up being the barber. He's fast with the draw and he is a sharpshooter with a rifle. We need a man like him with his experience and he is still only in his 40's. And he's always been with the posse. Now he wants to be a deputy."

Jimmy and Jericho agreed that Bronson should and would be an excellent deputy for Yuma. "He has a heart and only shoots in self-defense," Jimmy told Jericho.

"Bronson is married now. Her name is Sherry

and she is a beautiful woman, inside and out. She treats him like a king. Bronson is a very happy man being married."

Durango continued to speculate, "I think I am going to have Sindago as one of our deputies someday. We will need more deputies that are trained and you, Jimmy, and Sindago will go through training soon. Maybe both of you, depending on how wild it gets."

"I am going to miss working here at Yuma. Fast Eddie and Dixie are going to miss it too, I'm sure.

• • •

The next morning Durango was talking with Katie Joe, "It's Sunday... we should be heading out to the church. I don't want to miss Job's sermon. He is a very gifted man, and is blessed by God. This town is very fortunate to have him as the minister. That is why he has such a big congregation. He tells it like it is for people to understand and he takes it from the word. I don't know what I would do without Job; he has gotten me through some very difficult situations. Because of his prayers I have gotten through many things victoriously."

"I'll see you later Durango. I'm going to check on my diner."

Giving her a disapproving look, Durango said, "I'm sure everything is all right at the diner."

"But, because I am still the boss, I need to show up and check-in with my employees and to make sure there is no trouble," ending that discussion. But trying to reconcile, Katie Joe said, "How about we go swimming around 2 o'clock this afternoon?"

Durango smiled, "Sounds good, Katie Joe."

"We will have us some fun today."

"Unless it seems that I have more bad guys coming around causing trouble."

• • •

Durango was just getting back from church, and looking forward to going swimming with his darling, sexy wife to be. And after... he wanted to have some wild and crazy fun in bed with Katie Joe. She looked so hot in her tight jeans and low cut blouse and her long blonde hair with an erotic tan from swimming in the nude when nobody else was around.

He was walking to his horse Blazer when a loud voice from across the street called out his name. "Durango, do you remember me? I am Big Brawn. You sent me to prison for raping the teacher from New York. Charlotte was her name. She was the best I ever had. I like it when they put up a fight, it turns me on even more.

Big Brawn, seeing he had Durango's attention, went on, "I got a score to settle with you. Step out in the street or are you afraid that I am still as fast as a gunslinger as I used to be?"

Durango remembered how fast he was, recalling that he almost lost in a gunfight arresting him. He prayed to God to give him the speed he needed to put him down. Dead. Big Brawn stepped out into the street and he had the sun at his back.

Durango slowly walked out into the middle of the street. His blood was running as fast as the windy day that day. He could feel himself starting to shake and could smell death in the air. Durango thought that he just might meet his match that day. He was hoping that all the practice will pay off right now.

Big Brawn was cool as could be and knew that Durango was counting his blessings and seeing his life pass before his eyes.

Big Brawn went for his gun fast as lightning, Durango shot with both of his guns.

Durango just stood there after all the smoke had cleared. Big Brawn wasn't there. He was on the ground. Trying to stay alive squirming and screaming he aimed his gun at Durango. But Durango took a deep breath and shot Brawn again between the eyes. Durango fell to his knees and thanked the good Lord for the speed and that he was still alive.

Durango had met his match and won. "Today is another day, and I feel spiritually strong. A feeling of hope and joy all throughout my body. A sense of accomplishment from what went on today. I guess that is all I need to know."

And with that feeling of relief, he collapsed on the street.

• • •

"Are you ready to go swimming Durango? I have my swimsuit on underneath my pants." As he just laid there, Katie Joe exclaimed, "Durango, you have been shot!" Running to him, she yelled, "Someone, go get the doctor right away!"

Doc Levy came quickly. "Durango you have lost a lot of blood. You might not make it." He performed the surgery right on the street, extracting the bullet, and wrapping the wound.

He told Katie Joe, "It didn't hit any vital organs, but he has lost a lot of blood. Only time will tell if he lives or dies." Katie Joe just prayed. She was crying and holding him in her lap, rocking him back and forth telling him how much she loved him.

Convalescence

His room had that distinctive smell. The smell of a hospital room. He had lost so much fluids, the trauma of the gunfight and the loss of blood put Durango into a coma. He laid there motion less for days.

The first few days were touch and go. The next few days went by so slow for Katie Joe, to see him just lying there on the bed. All she could do was pray.

The doctor stopped by and told Katie Joe, "He may or may not live." Professional help was all he could give. He had nothing to give him for his coma. "But now he needs more. Durango has a warrior's spirit and it is possible that he might pull through."

He told her, "Talk to him and let him feel your love, Katie Joe. That will give him what he really needs right now to keep on fighting to stay alive."

Katie Joe had long feared that this day would come. She would have to be strong to endure seeing him like this. Her love for Durango was the only cure she could give to him right now.

Katie Joe was by his bed side morning, noon, and night. She read to him and prayed over him that he would pull through and come back to life.

She would tell him the stories of how they met, as kids, on the wagon train to Yuma. "It started out in 1800's when people were starting to make their way out west. People were fighting against all odds, starvation, lack of water, and Indian rampages. These people were only settlers; they had no idea of what they were getting themselves into."

"There were wagon trains that were organized and would take settlers out west. Remember Bronson?" she asked him. "Bronson was in charge of this wagon train heading west. He was true Grit, and was tough as nails and had been out west several times before. He knew all the journey was rough. There were no trails or roads to travel on. We had to make our way the best that Bronson knew how."

"The people that lived through the hard times got through it the best they could. If there were sicknesses, chances were slim to none that there was no doctors out there to help. They were out there all on their own traveling through the desert, and mountains, having to cross rivers and do whatever else that challenged them, for instance; wildlife that was looking for an easy meal."

• • •

Days turned into weeks. Close friends would stop by to visit him and talk to him. Job, and Samuel,

Jimmy, and even Jericho would stop in. Fast Eddie came by every couple of days. But the coma continued. He was so out of it, so far away, barely breathing and lifeless, and his friends wept to see him like that.

Katie Joe tried to rouse him. "You were only sixteen years old, traveling along with your mother and father, crossing over the rough terrain. You thought that your mom and dad had gone crazy to want to go west. But we got by. We talked a lot then. And you and Eddie and me, we tried to teach Betty Lou to read. And we'd eat blueberries. Oh, Durango, come back!"

• • •

Meanwhile, the town kept moving. Tricia brought in some breakfast for Jericho while he was cleaning his guns. "Got to keep them clean to keep them accurate," he said. "Remember, Tricia, keep the sun at your back."

She was enthralled. "Which hand is faster on the draw?" she wondered.

"They are both about the same." Seeing her interest, he said, "You know, I use to teach women how to shoot. I had a gun school just for women. I made a lot of money and met a few nice women along the way."

"I'd like that."

• • •

A few days later, Tricia was surprised to see Jericho in the diner again. "I'll be a monkey's uncle, you're not busy chasing down an outlaw today? Where is Mensa?"

"Oh, he had a night out last night. He's probably at the brothel hotel sleeping it off." He paused, but seeing no reaction, pressed on, "You have come a long way, Tricia. With your shooting. Remember to shoot from the hip. When you see them go for their gun, make your move and shoot for the heart."

Tricia was good… at the guns too. She shot with her guns just like Jericho showed her how to do it. You might say, that she was the fastest gun in the West when it comes down to women.

• • •

It was the first snowfall and Katie Joe was making breakfast for herself. The smell of the sausages and the smell of coffee freshly brewed seemed to awaken his senses. She went in to wish him a good morning with a kiss on the forehead and noticed that he moved his trigger finger on his right hand. It was the first sign of life from him in months. She got so excited. She pulled up a chair and whispered to him in his ear that she loved him. Then his eyes started to flutter. Then he slipped away back into his coma.

• • •

A few days later, Fast Eddie talked to him quietly saying, "Hey there old pal, how is it going? You know, the Durango City jailhouse is about finished. We're still going there, you and I, right?" Durango forced a smile on his face. It was another sign of life. Eddie quickly went to get Katie Joe and told her what had happened. She was beside herself. He had smiled. That was just topper.

She gave him a kiss on his forehead and said, "Welcome back my love!" She was so filled with joy, she started to cry. Fast Eddie wept to see his friend move with a smile. This time he didn't slip back into a coma.

Katie Joe knew he was going to live. It was just a matter of time now.

• • •

Later that day the Doctor came to see Durango. Katie Joe told him that he smiled and didn't slip back into the coma. He checked his blood pressure and said his heartbeat is getting stronger. His eyes were still dilated but the Doctor smiled and said, "He shows signs of life and is coming out of his coma. Just let him rest and talk to him. He'll pull out of this coma in a short while."

Onward

The day Durango was shot, Jimmy had been out- side of town. After his shift the day before, Jimmy had hopped onto his horse, Ringo, and headed off to Samuel and Shania's settlement. "I knew Sindago was going to be back there, after living with his grandfather for a while, to visit his mom and dad," he had told the deputies before leaving.

Sindago and Jimmy both had something in common. They both like to shoot their guns. Left or right handed made no difference which one. Sindago was further along in shooting bottles and cans. Jimmy could learn a lot from Sindago on how to draw a gun like a gunslinger. But both of them were the same age.

And in the west, being fourteen was old enough to go it alone. For Sindago, that meant no more bodyguards. Thunder and Lightning did not go along with Sindago to Shania and Samuel's. They had taken their own path, and he was old enough to be his own protector. The spirits have spoken, his grandfather had said. Sindago has learned about protecting himself, and he can come and go as he pleases on the reservation or wherever he wants to go.

But up to today, Sindago, was a grieving man. His grandfather had passed away. There's nothing that Sindago can do to bring himself back to being happy. He loved his grandfather very much.

Shania watched over Sindago and reminded him that he knew he was loved by Cuda. So, there will be time, sad times that Sindago had to face and to try to get along without his grandfather. Cuda had taught him many things about how he had lived as the chief of the Falling Rock Tribe; he had loved him like a close friend and father.

On the reservation, Sindago had become good friends with Angel. He had told Jimmy that he and Angel are truly lovers and friends and that they were always meant to be.

Angel knew that Sindago was suffering. There was nothing she could do to make him feel better. It was a time in Sindago's, life, for the first time he had felt all alone. His wisdom and his many other powers will have to see improvements in his life. He is the one that is chief and must endure this grieving alone. It will take time for him to get over this loss of his grandfather.

• • •

Shania had told Jimmy that Sindago was coming home that night. Jimmy was going to meet him at Samuel and Shania's house that night. He was hoping they were going to go and shoot bottles, like before. They were going to have themselves a lot of fun to see who was the best. Maybe that would cheer him up.

It was a good thing that Jimmy came along when he did. Sindago can grow with Jimmy. They can become good friends. Jimmy can teach him how to be happy again and be the man that he was meant to be. But he must conquer the loss of his grandfather that had loved him so much. It is Sindago's first loss of a loved one. He will be more of a man and realizing, Cuda's spirit will guide him through the rest of his life.

It will take weeks for Sindago to get over this death of his grandfather. But he will be stronger and wiser after he comes to grips with the loss. It is Sindago's first time dealing with sadness. But he will be wiser as a king to have gone through this. The tragedy of this Loss will only make him grow stronger. Sindago will get through this with Angel and Jimmy's help.

He will be happy again it will be just a matter of time.

• • •

As the months went by, Sindago had learned to deal with the loss of his grandfather and be happy again. Angel will be there for him through thick and thin. Jimmy will teach him how to be happy again just by being the best of friends.

Jimmy will be there for him to make him laugh again. They will go out and shoot guns, fish, and go out hunting and to teach him how to put the past behind and Carry On.

Sindago is learning to let go and to have learned a big lesson. Sindago laughs again and is horny again with his girl. He has gotten through and he has conquered his emotions of the loss.

• • •

Sindago is getting stronger by the day. He is discovering that death is a part of life. Sindago has gotten through it. And perhaps someday he can put that lesson toward learning to lead the Falling Rock Tribe like his grandfather did.

• • •

"It was a miracle," said Doctor Levy would later exclaim to anyone who would listen. "In all my years I have never seen this kind of turn-around from a man that should have died but has lived through something so close to death and lived. It is a miracle to behold."

But for now, Katie Joe sat by Durango holding his hand and telling him how much she loved him. He smiled again, and his breathing was stronger and more regular.

The doctor said, "I will leave the medicine for him for the pain, but otherwise he is doing much better and should be up and around in a week or so."

But he warned, "He may not be in reality for a while. Don't be alarmed with how he acts and what he says. He may be playing out what was happening before the gunfight. He will probably be delirious and may say things and imagine things that are not really happening, but that is to be expected for someone coming out of a deep coma. He'll be alright. Good bye, have a glorious day Katie Joe," the Doctor added cheerfully.

Durango had pulled through because he had a warriors' heart and the will to live because of the Love from Katie Joe and friends.

• • •

"You can go get the horses while I check on the diner before we leave town. Does that sound like a plan?"

Durango said, "It sounds like a great plan."

So he rounds up the horses and brings them down to the diner. "Get on Katie Joe we're going swimming. I need a bath and a good swim."

"So, do I," said Katie Joe.

"Maybe I'll do some fishing," said Durango. "We're going to have fun. I can't wait to see you in your swimsuit. I just bet it will knock me out."

Down at the pond Katie Joe said, "You're right, it is kind of tight."

"It fits me kind of tight. I have gained a little weight since I've been here working in the diner. But that's okay, right Durango?"

"You look fine Katie Joe and you sparkle like a diamond."

"Well thank you for the compliment."

"And it looks so right on such a beautiful woman as you."

"Where did you get all those muscles, Durango?"

"Building houses for a living. I got tired of it and moved into law enforcement. I see now that it is my calling to be sheriff of this town."

"Oh, look, Samuel caught a big bass. Shania also sells Indian pottery. He caught another one. I know what they're having for supper tonight. Let's have some chicken before it gets cold and some of that French bread. I've worked up an appetite, how about you Katie Joe?"

• • •

Katie Joe smiled as she looked down at Durango. "Eddie, he is in a fantasy world right now. The Doctor said that this may happen. He is coming out of his coma and is saying things that aren't really happening. But he is alive, and this fantasy world will take its course and he will be back to normal."

Fast Eddie told her not to worry: Jericho and a new deputy he hired, Mensa, kept the territory of Yuma as peaceful as possible.

Between Troy Harrison, the Mayor of Yuma, Jericho and Samuel, a new plan had been created for the railroad. It was a far better plan and the railroad companies would make lots of money going the route that the men had worked out for them. They can make Yuma a station that the trains could stop at for supplies. It would be a place where the Yuma farmers could sell their products to the railroad and make their fair share of the money.

Bringing in gold miners, settlers from out east and cowboys who like to work the farms. There was a prison in Yuma known for the rough and committed outlaws. For Yuma was settled there and the railroad trains and shipyards were all around the Yuma territory. It was a Godsend that the railroad stopped at Yuma, bringing in settlers and gamblers for the casino and where the railroad could pick up the farmers goods to sell further out west.

Every now and then a gunslinger would come into town looking for trouble. Jericho didn't take kindly for those kind of men hating the world and wanting to take it out on somebody. He, or his deputies, rode them out of town or a took care of them in a gunfight, whatever went down.

But Katie Joe wanted to get out of Yuma soon, because she didn't want to see anything trigger his emotions, or bring him back to the gunfight that almost killed him. She knew Yuma was known for train robbers, stagecoach robbers, bank robbers, and cold-hearted killers. Then there was the casino on the reservation that was a constant reminder of how greedy people can be. She thought, "we need a fresh start."

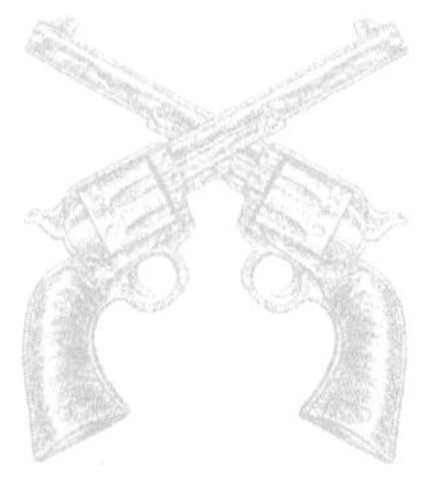

2Hole-in-the-Wall

It took another month, but as soon as he was strong enough to ride, Durango started out for Durango City. Jericho had already taken over as the master gunslinger sheriff of Yuma, and Fast Eddie was getting things started in Durango City. After sitting around healing, the boredom was killing Durango.

He needed to get back to work—Durango was still to be the new sheriff of Durango City. And none to soon: there was a rumor going around that robbers were going to steal the money off the train.

Samuel and his wife had come along to Durango City, and were helping Durango get things set up when they heard the news: there was a robbery on the train heading west with the bank roll of the Army's money.

Although there were soldiers on the train, the robbers used dynamite and killed all of the soldiers and stole the money. Samuel's wife, Shania, was a tracker—taught to her by her father Cuda. With her help, the lawmen got on the chase when

Shania followed the robbers tracks to their hide-out—she led them right to where they were splitting the money. It was only three men that had robbed the train, because of the dynamite.

It didn't take long, seeing as how they surprised the robbers, who didn't think anyone could find them so quickly. One outlaw had died when a sharpshooter took him out. "The other two thieves will hang once the judge hears what happened," said Durango. "Gather up the money and I'll bring it back to the General of the Army."

Once they were back in town, Durango told his posse, "Drinks and dinner are on me at the Big Top Diner for all the brave men," and looking at Shania, "...and women, who helped getting the money back."

• • •

After listening to his tale, Katie Joe said, "Samuel invited us over for fish tonight, if you're interested."

"I promised the boys in the posse that they can have free drinks and dinner on the house."

She said, "That they deserve it."

"I'll have to take a buggy to carry all this money to the General. Won't he be happy that he got all of his money back? It was a good day."

"That sounds like a great idea. I'll see you around six tonight."

Durango turned to his deputy and said, "Shiloh,

you watch over the other two thieves in the jailhouse until I return."

● ● ●

Durango grabbed one of the other deputies to help him load the buggy and prepare the horse's harness. And after a short ride, he rode into the Army's encampment a couple miles outside of town.

Without so much of an announcement, he walking into the makeshift headquarters. "Here you go General, all your money is there."

The General was stunned. "So quickly?"

"Well that's what I do. I keep order around here. So, when are you leaving for Mexico, General?"

"I'll be leaving in a few weeks. Thank you for putting up with us in your town."

"You were no trouble at all. Some of your men got a little rowdy but that's to be expected. And now that they have some money, I suppose we'll be seeing more of them in town?"

"Yes, I guess you will sheriff. But I'll tell them to behave. Or you might take their money back! Hah!" After chucking to himself, the General added congenially, "Have a good evening Durango and I'll see you in town, soon."

● ● ●

After the ride back from the Army camp, Durango

got down to business. Back at the jailhouse, he sent the deputy over for some food for the thieves.

Pulling up a chair by the jail cell, Durango asked the men, "Don't you know that you're going to hang for stealing that money? It's a federal offense."

Grunts was all Durango got in response.

He pressed on, "But there might be another option. I'm looking for the Jesse James gang. If you can help me find them, maybe the judge will go easy on you. They were in the hole in the wall hideout the last I heard of them. Do you know where the hole in the wall is?"

"Yes, we do," said one of the men from the jail cell.

"You know, there are a lot of bad guys at the hole in the wall. You would be doing us a big favor and saving your lives by turning them in. What do you say about that? Would you take me there along with several of my deputies?"

Seeing the opportunity, the men eagerly said, "Yes, we will do that. We will help you to get to the hole in the wall."

"How far of a ride is it?"

"About five hours from here."

"Fine, we'll take off tomorrow around 11:00 AM. I reckon we'll have about 30 deputies coming along. Plenty enough to watch you two, and take care of James and his gang."

Seeing their agreement, he continued, "What we will have to do is plan to attack."

"The camp is surrounded by steep rock walls.

They have lookouts, and fire shots in the air if they see lawmen heading towards the hole in the wall."

"So, what we got to do is take them out by silence." Durango continued to test the men, "Do you know where the lookouts are stationed?"

"Yes, we know where most of them are, Durango."

"They are very bad outlaws that live in the hole in the wall. But we are very good lawmen. When we get there, you will show us where the lookouts are, and we will take them down. We'll sneak up to the lookouts and shoot them with a bow and arrow or use a knife on them. They will not know that we are coming for them."

Durango added, "Then we will have our sharp-shooters positioned strategically around on the rocks."

"We'll attack in early morning. The lookouts will have a little fire going so we will be able to spot them easily. After all the lookouts have been taken out, we'll go in for the kill." Passing a paper and pencil into the cell, Durango continued, "Draw us a map of what the hole in the wall looks like inside, so, we will know how to plan our attack."

Seeing the food had arrived, he concluded, "Well, get some rest after you're done eating because it's going to be a long day tomorrow."

• • •

The next morning, Durango rouses the prisoners.

"It's 11:00 AM and we are headed out to the hole in the wall. You thieves ride up front with me."

• • •

It was a long, but uneventful, ride out to the area just outside where the James gang were hiding. They were hidden from view, protected by also blind. Durango was saying to Fast Eddie, "Our scouts know who they are going to take out, silently and deadly." And to the prisoners, "I have the map that you have given me. We will wait till morning, after all the lookouts have been taken out, and then we'll know if you were telling the truth. If so, we will charge in full force and catch them by surprise."

Fast Eddie agreed, "The plan should work successfully. If they don't know that we are there, we will win."

"Is everybody ready, are your guns full of ammunition? This is a one time chance. We cannot fail. We're going in for the kill at the break of dawn," Durango told the posse.

"Let us go over the plan of attack one more time," said Fast Eddie, wanting to be sure. "The sharpshooters will take out the ones getting on their horses and hiding behind rocks. We will attack the ones out in the open shooting at us. One shot, one kill. They are very good shooters and we must catch them by surprise."

Everyone was in agreement. So the plan was put

into action. As part of the team disappeared into the night, Durango told the rest, "The scouts have left to do their job. It is nightfall and they will suspect nothing until it's too late for them. For the rest of us, we wait."

• • •

A few tense but quiet hours later, Durango whispers, "It is about sunup and it is time to get ready to attack. Everything is going according to plan." Looking around at the shadowy faces of his posse, he asks, "Is everybody ready? Because we're taking off into the hole in the wall in a few minutes, and we're counting on each of you men to do your job."

If the men were afraid, they didn't show it. In fact, everyone was eager to make this happen. Durango said, "Good. It is time to go!"

The horses took off at an explosive speed headed into the hole in the wall. The deputies had their pistols shooting, giving everything inside no chance to survive. The bad men were going down like a turkey shoot. They had no chance of recourse but to run and get shot down.

Some stayed in the caves but were taken out by the sharpshooters. Durango's men used dynamite and rapid shooting. After about twenty minutes, it was all over.

Durango was proud of his men. As the smoke settled, he told them all, "It is all over and said and done. We went in there to do what we had to do, and we did it the way we had planned it. Success was ours." Glancing at the two train robbery prisoners who had helped make this attack a success, he continued, "There are still more outlaws that were not in there at the time we attacked. Lucky for them, I suppose. They will live to do crime another day."

"But we'll catch them some other time," said Fast Eddie.

• • •

On the ride back to Durango City, Durango talked quietly with his friend, "It has been a long couple of days, Fast Eddie. It was a miracle that none of our deputies were injured on the raid. I thank God for that. He has really been my source of miracles these past few weeks. I feel so full of his spirit, I feel like I am about to explode with joy for the victory and the joyfulness I feel inside."

Many outlaws met their match that day. Those that survived would earn their way to the gallows. The trials were short, and it was all over in a few days. All the outlaws from the hole in the wall were dead, either on the spot or wounded and later hanged.

Reporting back to his deputies after the trials, Durango said, "The thieves that helped us with the ambush were given a pardon by the judge. It's fair. I just hope they stay out of trouble now that they have a second chance."

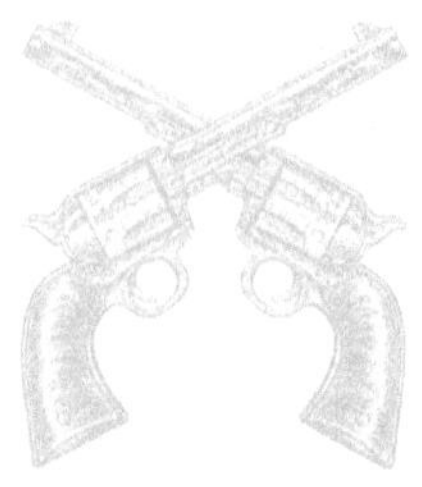

Pinkerton Detective Agency

News of the end of Jesse James and his gang spread around the west quickly. It wasn't long before an outlaw that hadn't been at the hole in the wall at the time of the raid came around Durango City looking for revenge.

Deputy Shiloh was making his rounds about town when a shot rang out without warning. And just like that, the outlaw had killed their deputy. Shot him in the back.

But the outlaw didn't hang around. He disappeared into the night. No justice could be served.

Even though he had suspected something like it might happen, Durango was saddened by shooting. And frustrated by the cowardice of the outlaw. Shiloh was a good man and a great deputy.

At the service for the slain lawman, Durango got up and said, "Somebody shot my deputy for revenge of what our lawmen did to the hole in the wall gang. Shiloh will be missed, but not forgotten." Everybody in town was there at the funeral.

He was buried with his guns and his badge. "May he rest in peace," sighed Durango.

• • •

A while back, some of Durango's deputies decided to establish the Pinkerton Detective Agency. Their goal was to solve crimes that crossed jurisdictions, and that a town Sheriff and other law enforcement couldn't solve. They were very intelligent and scientifically solved murders.

The men of the Pinkerton Agency were trained detectives with forensic science training in Universities from across the world who had banned together to solve cold murders. They were especially known for solving mysterious killings, and locating hard to find high ranking killers.

They worked for an agency that was taught to gather evidence to put the worst of the worst behind bars and also many were to be executed. Although they started out in Yuma, they spread worldwide.

Durango called them in to solve the mystery of the death of Shiloh.

• • •

"Where were they standing when they saw the murder happen?"

"They heard some rumbling from their house and looked out to see what was going on?"

"There was a fist fight between Shiloh and the

murderer and the killer killed him with a knife, slashing him right across the throat."

"That is the truth, so help me God."

Stories were rampant, and wide spread accounts were contradictory. But through careful work, the detectives determined it was about 10:30 at night and the deputy was doing his rounds. "We suspect the outlaw came out of an alley and took him by surprise and killed Shiloh."

Through deduction, they tracked down Shiloh's murderer.

With some eye witnesses that picked the man out from a wanted poster they were on his trail and found him in a town working on the chain gang from a rape charge doing time in Yuma prison. It was the outlaw Mac Caine, who had a list of murders a mile long. "We just needed good evidence to finally pin one on him."

Now he faced the murder charge of killing Shiloh if the witnesses would identify him as the lone killer. But the eye witnesses were scared if he broke out of prison that they would be next on his list to kill. The agency had to convince them that they would be safe because he was in solitary confinement for being accused of murdering a lawman. He would be in solitary confinement the rest of his life if convicted.

TEN MEN IN YUMA

Life was getting back to normal for the residents of Durango City. No one had tried to cross his now famous deputies, and the jail had been mostly empty since the trials. Durango was appreciative, but restless. He decided to pay his friends in Yuma a visit, and fill them in on the apprehension of the notorious gang.

It was decided that he would take Katie Joe along, and they were going to stay with Samuel and Shania for a couple of days.

• • •

Down in Yuma, Mensa came into the jailhouse and said, "Good morning!" Durango had been catching up with the deputies he knew from before, but they all turned and said good morning to Mensa.

"Mensa, I want you to meet Sheriff Durango. This used to be his town, up until a few months ago when he headed up to be the lawman of Durango City." Jericho was proud of this new deputy, and

Durango could tell he wanted to make sure he would settle in for a long time.

After the men greeted each other, Jericho continued with his plans for Mensa, "I'll want to find you a farm close by the town, so you don't have to live in that hotel/brothel much longer. You've lived there quite a while and didn't complain. I think it's about time we find you a farmhouse. There is a really, nice farmhouse just east of town. You and Gracie can move in together and start a family. She would like that," Jericho added with a wink.

Gracie had taken to helping feed the deputies, and she wasn't going to be overlooked. "I brought some breakfast for you too Mensa. Some fine French buttermilk pancakes with lots of butter and maple syrup and some juicy sausages."

Durango was still catching up with his old friends. "Hey Jimmy. I haven't seen you around in quite a while. Where have you been?"

"I've been going to school learning my ABC's," Jimmy replied.

Durango was skeptical, but Gracie thought it was great, saying, "Maybe someday you'll grow up to be a doctor or a lawyer or maybe even a banker."

"Thank you, Gracie, maybe I will!" But for now, Jimmy knew he had work to do. "Mensa, would you like your horse groomed today?"

"That would be just terrific Jimmy."

Once things settled down, Jericho continued with his real estate deal. "Mensa, what do you say we go look at that farmhouse out of the east of town? I think you would like it and so will Gracie. A two-bedroom house and acres of land. It has a stable for your horses a barn for your hay and the little shack that you could use either to store items or make it a workshop. Has a fenced in area for your horses to run and a well for your water."

"And the price is right," added Jericho. "It's only a rocks throw away from the main street. Just a short distance away from the jailhouse if anything should happen here in town. What do you say Mensa?"

"Sure, as soon as Jimmy is done grooming my horse."

"We'll head over right before lunch. You know he'll never leave you alone now that you let start grooming your horse," Jericho said with a smile.

• • •

"What do you think of the home Mensa? Is it all what I said it was?" Jericho was excited to make sure he liked it.

Mensa said, "It is a fine home, and I'm sure Gracie would love it."

"If you need furniture I know someone who has extra. And I ended up with more pots and pans than I need. Let's take a look inside and see what you think? He said, it is right nice in here. Plenty of room and a nice fireplace."

Looking around inside, Mensa said, "Yes Jericho, I like it, but I'll have to get Gracie's approval too. But I'm sure she'll love it."

"Well I'm glad. Let's head back to town and you can tell Gracie all about it. I'm going to go to the Big Top anyhow to get me a steak and potato. You let me know if you want it and I'll set you up with the owner to work out a price. Since Gracie is working at the Big Top, maybe you can grab lunch with me and ask Gracie at the same time?"

"That sounds like a plan to me, Jericho."

• • •

On the way back into town, Jericho and Mensa meet up with Durango. While they are chatting, several men from out of town ride past them. "Look Durango, we got some strangers riding into town. Do you know any of them?"

"Any of them on wanted posters?" Mensa eagerly asks.

"We'll just have to see, Mensa."

"It looks like they're going into the Big Top Diner for a bite to eat, too," said Durango. "I can hear Teddy playing his piano and singing—I see he still plays and get the girls singing and dancing to entertain the cowboys."

"I used to always sit by the window, so I can keep an eye on things going on in town," said Durango.

"I'm sure you're old table is still available," says Jericho as they walk in.

• • •

Tricia said, "What's it going to be boys, the usual?"

"You bet, you sweet love of mine," said Jericho. Durango noticed Jericho had a new fling going. As they found their table, Jericho speaks low to the other two men, "One of those cowboys looks like a gunslinger. If he has no wanted poster and starts no trouble, he is fine by me."

"But he's going over to the game table," observes Mensa. "It looks like he's got a lot of money."

Durango notes, "The other two are eating the steak and potatoes like they haven't eaten for a week."

"The food is delicious here. That's why they eat like they do."

"Maybe..."

But Mensa didn't want to wait to see what happened. "I'm going to go check to see the wanted posters at the jailhouse and see if there is a match."

"Okay Mensa, but I'm going to sit here and eat my meal. Before you go, be sure to ask Gracie about the house."

"I almost forgot. But I'll ask her when I get back." As he turns to leave, he adds, "After we're done here let's go do some target practice."

"Sound good to you Mensa?"

"Yeah that sounds good to me."

• • • •

Mensa came back from the jailhouse and said, "One of them looks like Roy Roberts. A bank robber who rode with the hole in the wall gang."

"Well, alright." Putting down his fork, Jericho continues, "Go arrest him Mensa, I got your back."

For clarity, he adds, "He is the one playing cards with all the money." Mensa tries to casually walk around the room over to behind where Roberts is sitting. "Roy, you're under arrest. Don't reach for your gun. We got you all covered."

But he is unfazed. "We have got 10 cowboys riding into town tomorrow. Most of them are gunslingers." Continuing to play cards, he casually looks back at the barrel of Mensa's gun, saying, "So, let's just forget about the wanted poster and let us go about our business."

"You're under arrest Roy. You can go quietly or rowdy. Makes no difference to me."

Tossing down his cards in disgust, he casually says, "Okay I'll go quietly. But the 10 cowboys tomorrow... you'll have to settle with them."

"Get up and let's go. NOW!" commanded Mensa.

Jericho joins him, adding loudly enough for everyone to hear, "Your friends at the bar have no bounty or posters out on them. Long as they behave themselves they won't be arrested."

"That's it, get up nice and easy and walk to the door," says Mensa. He leads him across the street and into the jailhouse. The other deputies are ready. "Take that cell over in the corner.

That's where you'll be doing time until the judge gets here."

Durango was concerned about Roy's lackadaisical attitude. Once he was sure nothing else would happen, he went to the jailhouse and told Mensa, "The other two cowboys must've left town to warn the other cowboys about the trouble here in Yuma and that we arrested Roy and he is doing time for his crime. Round up 10 lawmen for tomorrow, because it looks like it's going to be a showdown."

"We'll be ready for them with our sharpshooters on the roof tops and the others will be behind us. They will be hiding where they can't be seen. I am going to go do some target practice and I'll be back in a while," Mensa said.

Durango said, "Okay. I'll stay here and keep an eye on Roy."

Mensa was telling the other men, "It looks like there is going to be some trouble tomorrow. We've seen trouble before and tomorrow will be just another day. I'll see you when I get back. If there is any trouble in the meantime, just fire two shots."

• • •

Sure enough, the next day the gunslingers rode into town looking for Roy. As Roy said, it was 10 cowboys, and clearly they thought that they would intimidate the lawmen to set their buddy loose.

Mensa, Jericho, and Durango stood in the

middle of the main street. Roy was in the jailhouse, behind them. The otherwise empty street let the gunslingers know that they weren't getting Roy without a fight.

So, they got off their horses and proceeded to walk down Main Street towards the jailhouse. All the lawmen's sharpshooters were in place on the roof tops, wagons and corners of buildings. Watching closely.

"We don't want any trouble. We just want Roy. We have gunslingers that can out shoot your men very easily. Let's settle this peacefully and give us Roy and we'll be on our way."

"Roy is an outlaw and stands to be tried and punished for his crime. If you don't leave now, there will be trouble." Jericho continued, "So, why don't you get on your horses and ride out of town."

The gunslingers lined up across the street. When the lawmen saw them go for their guns, they fired on the outlaws. There was smoke everywhere gunpowder filled the air and the gunslingers dropped like flies.

With only one outlaw left standing, Durango and the gunslinger squared off. The gunslinger drew first. But Durango was faster, shooting with both guns and firing till the gunslinger fell dead to the ground.

Some of the lawmen were injured but for the most part they were victorious. The deputies started cleaning up and tending to their wounded. Durango and Mensa walked back to the jailhouse and stepped in only to find Roy pleading for his life with Jericho.

"You have one chance to live and that is to turn in another hideout, other than the hole in the wall. I can't say that the judge will pardon you for all that you have done. Do you know of another hideout Roy?"

Roy pleaded, "I can help you find Black Bart's hideout. He's the most notorious stagecoach robber there ever was. He's staying at a mountain house in California. It's about 9 miles north of Berry Canyon on Oro-Quincy highway. I can take you to the hideout in Black Hills range in New Mexico. This place ought to be enough to pardon me from the gallows."

Seeing Jericho had it all under control, Durango said he was going to gather up Katie Joe and hit the trail, that it was time to head back to his own town of Durango City.

The next day the judge came to town and checked into his favorite brothel. What with the information on Black Bart, he sentenced Roy to only six months in Yuma prison. "It could have been a hanging, he got off easy," said Mensa.

• • •

"I am starving. Lets go to have us some dinner." Durango was still restless after the visit with his friends down in Yuma. So he and his deputies went across the street for dinner.

• • •

"Here are your steaks, boys, fresh from the grill with onions broiled to perfection and vinaigrette topped with French seasonings sure to hit the spot." Katie Joe said to Durango, "That was sure a good fish fry at Samuel's house last night. Shania looks like she is pregnant. A second child. No wonder Samuel is so happy."

"They make good parents," Job said. The preacher had joined them on the ride back to Durango City, and was sitting with Durango and the deputies that were on duty that night.

Katie Joe said, "I want children too."

Anticipating this, Durango said, "I would rather wait a few more years before raising a family."

Katie Joe was still happy, adding before heading back to the kitchen, "All I want is a family someday."

Seeing the look on Job's face, Durango told him, "Whenever Katie Joe is ready to have children, that will be fine with me."

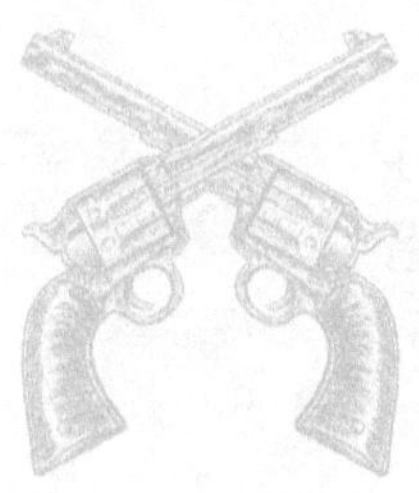

Gunslinger Jimmy

Jimmy takes being a deputy really seriously. Junior or not, he is becoming a better deputy every day. He is practicing shooting bottles and getting faster at the draw and he is getting stronger working on the farm. Jericho is teaching him how to be a lawman. And Jimmy has found himself a new girlfriend, Isabella.

•   •   •

One night, Jimmy was at work at the jailhouse, overseeing the town of Yuma. From across the street at the Big Top Diner he heard some gunshots. Jimmy ran over to see what the commotion was. It was three rustlers shooting up the diner. Jimmy took out his guns and warned them to settle down.

They said, "You're no lawman, you are just a boy."

Jimmy said, "Put your guns away or I am going to shoot all three of you."

"They said, so you want a gunfight? Let's, take it outside, boy."

The three lined up outside and said, "C'mon boy show us what you got." One of the three drew first and the gun fight was on.

Jimmy shot them all down.

He couldn't believe he did that! The townspeople were excited for Jimmy. Jimmy said, "Get them bodies off the street. They are dead meat."

Jericho came out of the jailhouse and said. "You shot them three cowboys all by yourself? Good job Jimmy! You're an official gunslinger. How does it feel Jimmy?"

Jimmy knew it then. He is now a gunslinger.

"You just shot three rustlers dead." Turning to the townsfolk who had started to gather, "Time to get Gideon the undertaker over here to clean up the mess."

Isabella, who had been helping wait tables at the Big Top after closing up the candy shop, ran out into the street and asked Jimmy, "Are you alright?" She was in shock from the encounter inside, but was as excited as he was that Jimmy had just shot down the three outlaws. She knew what this meant for him.

Clapping him on the back, Jericho said, "Durango and fast Eddie are going to be, so proud of you."

Isabella lead Jimmy back into the jailhouse to sit down. Jimmy couldn't even believe it. "I guess I am a gunslinger. I guess all my practice paid off."

Jericho had followed them in and said, "Now you're ready to be a real deputy."

Jimmy said, "Wait till Sindago hears about this? He's going to be so proud of me. It just had COME so easily. I guess I am a gunslinger through and through it's what I'd do."

● ● ●

The next morning, Jimmy meets up with Isabella. Jimmy likes to call her Isabell, and she thinks that is cute. Like him. But after all the excitement the previous night, she is horny as hell. And Jimmy is at that age and can't seem to get enough....

They like going swimming naked down at the pond. And going on long rides with their horses. And they like to eat at the Big Top Diner. They like going to carnivals and rodeos and they like moonlit walks together.

But they are both serious about the future. Jimmy is still going to school and wants to become the Sheriff someday when he graduates. He may even want to be mayor of Yuma. And Isabella, when she isn't working at the candy shop, is going to school to become a lawyer.

But the future could wait just one more day. Tonight would be right to celebrate Jimmy's first. The townspeople would have a party at the pole barn. Jimmy was fast with two guns. Didn't matter which one. One of the town of Yuma's own sons would become deputy.

The jamboree was at 8:30 and there the lawmen will be. Sindago will be there to party with the rest and to bring Angel, "the finest wife that could ever be."

Jericho gave a little speech, "Now look at all these lawmen who protect the town."

And Jimmy boldly added, "To any would-be trouble makers, If you don't want to die, then don't come around!"

• • •

But the jubilation never lasts long in the west.

"First thing they do when they get in the town is head for the saloon. Nothing on their mind except for them to drink their whiskey and start some trouble," growled Jimmy to the other lawmen. Three shady looking figures had just ridden in, joined by a handful of others, hardly even looking at the festivities.

Shrugging, Mensa said, "They look like friendly cowboys to me." "Let's just see how much trouble they make. But I think they're just passing through. No need to worry. Let's concentrate on having a jamboree."

"Zack is up for murder you know. We got to watch him close to make sure his buddies don't come after him. Today is his court trial so it might have a little bit of trouble there."

"You figure that's why they're here in town, huh?"

Jericho added, "You know we get all kinds that come through this town, so just relax."

"I don't know. The one dressed in black he looks like a gunslinger."

"Well, we just wait and see won't we."

Jericho conceded, "Mensa go get Samuel and let him know we got some outlaws in town. You know it might be that gang that is here for Zack before the trial. And tell everyone to keep an eye out and make sure that there is no trouble. We got to protect the judge and make sure he is safe."

"There's 9 of them and only four of us but we've been in bigger gunfights than this. The first person we shoot will be the one dressed in black. He's got trouble written all over. Courts at high noon and then we'll see if we're going to have a gunfight or not?"

"Go round up the other deputies so we got them out numbered."

"That ought to put a stop to them in a heartbeat. Let's tell them to move on, they're not wanted here in Yuma."

"I'll go for the one in black," said Jericho.

"They are coming out of the bar and they look like they are lining up down Main Street like they want to gunfight."

"Well there's 9 of them and now there's five of us. But we can handle them. They're not going anywhere alive, got that right Jimmy?"

"You got that right, Jericho."

"When they go for their guns let the party begin."

"Remember, that I got the one in black," said Jericho.

The man in black said, "All we want is our friend out of jail. There is going to be no hanging today."

"Well we'll see about that won't we, Jimmy?"

All, of a sudden, guns started blazing. The other cowboys went down while the man in black was still standing. Jericho said, "It's you and me. Take your best shot, because you're going down."

The man reached for his pistol but that's all he did. He went down just like all the rest.

Rodeo in Yuma

Just about that time Katie Joe rides into town with Dixie. They had been riding all day to get to Yuma, but had gone for a swim, and hadn't heard the commotion. "What happened here Jericho?"

"We had a shoot-out. They wanted that man in jail and they were willing to die for him. One of our man got shot but he's, okay."

"He'll still be good for the party?"

"The bullet only grazed his shoulder. So, he'll be ready to dance with any single women." Looking down at the man in black, Jericho said, "I was the lucky man he was the fastest shooter. But I shot him down."

Then Jericho ordered, "Now get this mess cleaned up, so we can have us a jamboree out in the middle of Main Street where everybody can come and go and party!"

• • •

The name of the rodeo is called "Wild Child Rodeo"

and it is known throughout the west. Held in Yuma every year on the 4th of July weekend, it was an event that Durango, Katie Joe, Fast Eddie and Dixie didn't want to miss. And the jamboree that lead up to it was always a good time.

As the posters all over town said, "If you like good fun, bring your friends along ,because the rodeo is meant to be big and strong."

That is where Fast Eddie met up with Dixie— where she "pulled out the wolf in Fast Eddie," noted Katie Joe. It was love at first sight between those two, and they still danced to the music all night long.

All of the townspeople danced to the music and all kinds of relationships were started that night. They were celebrating because the 4th of July was in two days, and it was a starlit night with a full moon shining bright.

The party was still in full force when Durango and Katie Joe snuck out. They wanted to go to their room at the Saloon and have the party of their own. The jamboree always got Katie Joe really hot, and she could not wait to get home with Durango.

Durango didn't relax much, but when it did it always put Katie Joe in a sexual mood. They left the party so Durango could take care of Katie Joe, and fire up her every need. Durango could satisfy Katie Joe all day and all night.

And the jamboree just partied on. There was dancing and romance and all night long under the full Moon. Yuma was a partying town. Sometimes they just had to deny all the bad things that go on.

• • •

The jamboree was just a lead up to the rodeo on the 4th of July in Yuma. Everybody was looking towards that. The bucking Broncos they come out of it shoots mad as hell as the bronco try to get the rider off of its back. The cowboys had to stay on the saddle on the back of the bronco for 8 seconds.

But the judge scores him on their rides of the bronco. The riders get broken bones from their rides. But the next time that they have that turned a ride they get back on the horse or bull and ride again. It's a tough life. The riders are in it for the fortune and fame. They have rodeo clowns that try to distract the bulls and keep them from seeing the riders that they don't get hurt. Some will ride the bronco some will lose, and it depends on the judge to see how he rode his bronco.

Back in the broncos booth, the cowboys try to make the broncos mad so that they put on a good show in front of the crowd. "That bronco being the meanest of all of the rest of them, and all hard it would be for the cowboy to get a toehold on. They get them as bulls in the first place. The ones that got anger written all over them. The bulls after they draw the cowboy on the ground they try to stab them with their horns or take them out with their back legs.

The bull riders wear flak jackets so it they are bucked off it doesn't hurt as bad and it causes bendable injuries. "But some I've seen," Fast Eddie was telling Dixie, "have known to get broken ribs. Or even a broken back."

They have horse races, barrel races, and many other races they do with the horses. They trained them horses' to go fast around the barrels and just straight lines to see how fast they can go. It's a tough way to make a living, but some people believe in their bones that they just have to do that. Something inside them drives them to keep riding.

Then there is a rope drawing to see how fast you are. The first they send out the sheep to see if they can pull them down and how fast they can do it. It is a sport not like any other. Cowboy against animal.

The rodeo is a fun show. It is great for everybody at all ages. "I'm there for the fireworks after the rodeo," said Dixie.

• • •

When the show ended, Jimmy turned to Katie Joe and Durango and said, "It was a great night for the fireworks!"

"They were Topper," Katie Joe agreed.

"Well, how do you do like the rodeo?" asks Jimmy.

"Maybe next year the Wild Child Rodeo will be in Durango City," wondered Durango.

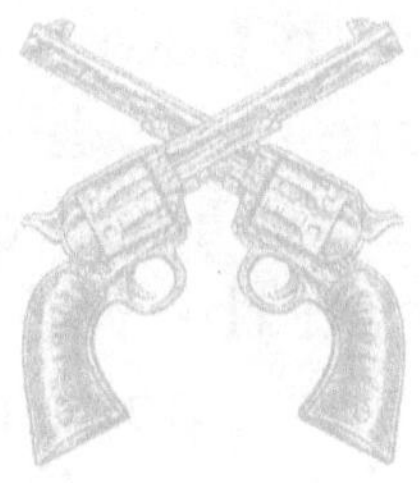

ᏢROGRESS IS ᏚPELLED ᎠIAGO

Back in Durango City, Durango and Fast Eddie were watching the town in action. "Well, there is Diago. That man is interested in being a lawman."

"He a man we can trust?" Eddie asked Durango.

Durango said, "The mob won't get him. He is wealthy, investing in the telephone and the new power lines. They are using Cedar and poles other than pine, so they will last a very long time."

And it was true. There were no more power outages. Durango knew Diago is making money hand over fist with his investments. "It is not what you got it is what you do with what you got," Diago had once told him.

"Diago knows Karate and knows how to shoot his guns, too. I am glad he is on our side. That is the truth," Durango added.

"I wish I got in on the ground floor like he did," Eddie was saying. "Everybody didn't think that telephone would be such a winner or electricity all around town."

The train lines and the progress of the ships and

barges that keeps the money rolling in daily for investors. Just had to take a chance sometimes and look at the future and where it is going. Diago was one man that seen it all coming. It is called progress. Now he is in the roll of dough. He is set for life and no worries about money for him. He don't act rich but the man is rich and powerful when it comes to investments.

"Talk to him and find out what the next thing would be to invest in. I bet he will say automobiles," chuckled Durango.

But it was a time for change. Henry Ford is working on his own project here in the states. Henry ford has a model A that he is working on. While over in Germany they are mastering an automobile that may out do our cars here in this country.

"I think that Diago is investing in the automobiles in Germany. He is a well-rounded man. He keeps himself in shape with Karate and practices his firearms out in the land he owns out in the country."

He goes to church. Not on a regular basis but he goes because his investors like to see him go. They would be doubtful of him if he didn't have a faith. You know how suspicious people are when you are handling their money. He has a brilliant business minded girlfriend that helps him out if he has a question about his business. She is an accountant. She watches over his money and investments. She also does his taxes for him.

"He wants to be a lawman because his father was a captain of the law. So he grew up seeing how the law works," and he can use his expertise of his karate sometimes when needed, or to shoot his gun and derringer when needed, thought Durango. He is doing alright for himself.

Durango knew he and Eddie are lucky to have him on the force.

• • •

From then it was only history of the Kitty Hawk that progressed to what we have today. But Diago became a very rich man investing in the future. He had his hands in almost everything.

Now he was to be a lawman working for the likes of Durango and Eddie. Jimmy and Sindago would be another addition to the Durango City law enforcement, as soon as Durango could get them up here. Diago had his hands in the trains heading from the east to the west. Carrying supplies from the east and settlers and passengers heading out west.

There was nothing he couldn't do. Diago had a great portfolio but an untried experience in law enforcement. He was the one who helped Durango in managing the law. Putting together a sound and well together school for future policemen to learn law enforcement. Durango and the rest needed more education because of the criminals were more sophisticated in carrying out their crimes.

It was still the wild west and the need for more training was evident. The crimes were trying their hardest to outdo the police training. Trying to buy off the lawmen was for most on their minds and would have made it simpler for them to carry out their wicked ways. But the laws were clear and had punishment worse than the criminals if they crossed the line.

• • •

They were cleaning up the town, and it wasn't just gunslingers. All of the mobsters that were busted on that one day, congressmen, bought judges, crooked lawmen, and all that were on the take would never work in law enforcement again anywhere. The punishment was stiff—for one thing they were put in the prisons with the outlaws. Those were some of the punishments and many more.

They hired only those whose background check had to come up clean without any incidence against the law.

They hired thirty after the school training was completed. The training was like marine corps boot camp. It was tough to get through, but those who had made it through were paid a good salary and treated with the utmost respect.

They were taught hand to hand combat, karate, rifle and intense gun training. They were taught the new ways of robberies and underground training. They were taught forensics and how to do a stake out. They were fully trained in the ways of the common outlaws and the new organized criminals.

Thy still rode horses. The cars were not popular yet. There was a big stable for the horses. They had to groom their own horses and feed them and to ride them to keep them in shape. When they graduated they were issued uniforms.

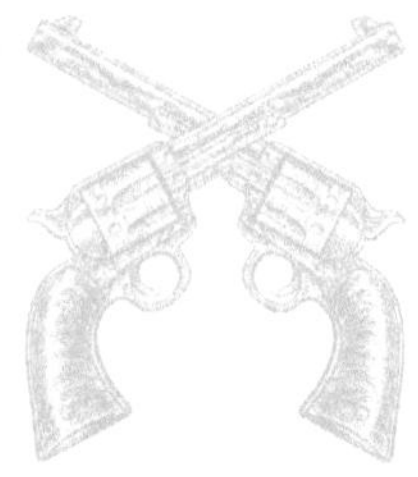

The Next Adventure

It was a busy town people moving in by the train loads to start in Durango City. It was a land of opportunity that had spread coast to coast after the Civil War.

However, opportunity doesn't always mean progress. There was the casino that Durango planned on sending Jimmy and Sindago to, where they will be able really shine—they will be in charge of 26 officers and the casino will only be open till ten o'clock. It will open at six in the morning and go all day into the evening.

And there was drugs being shipped in on the boats. They were headed east and west.

Diago was as angry about this corruption as the long-time lawmen. So he called a meeting with Eddie and Durango. They discussed plans on how to take down the mob. How the information was going to be gathered, who was going to go in, who would be second to relay the information.

"That will leave the other fifteen men to patrol the

streets. I want my best walking the streets, looking for trouble," Durango said.

Eddie agreed, "We want the ones who have streets smarts out on the streets."

Durango, Fast Eddie and Diago were planning their next moves to get ahead of the crime. "We are needing one person to go underground, undercover. Eddie I pick you," says Diago.

Durango looked at Eddie, and he knew he could do it. "It will be a dangerous job if you take it, Eddie."

"I'll need extra training for this assignment."

"You will get all you need, don't worry about that," said Diago.

"Will there be anybody that could ID you?" Durango asked.

Diago continued the briefing, "They are coming in from the east so chances of knowing him would be slim to none. We got a good shot at this, Eddie. And Durango will be pulled in to help as soon as you have earned their trust."

"This should go off like diamonds in the rough. There will be a lot of questions for you, so study up on their ways. Don't look to polished, just enough to get by. Bring out your street smarts, you will need them. They are going to be looking at you close. Remember your lies and what is real. Keep your wits about you Eddie."

"You will be on your own. Every other day you will be reporting to Durango on the sly. You will meet somewhere at a brothel where men come and go. If there is any sign of danger that you can't handle get out of there right away. Or you call when you can. I'll take all of your calls."

"But if we haven't heard from you in three days, we're going in," Durango adds.

"Yes," Diago says, "But while you are in there, you will be the only one in there. Don't let any-one tell you different. Durango will be your partner and that is it. There will be no change in the plan. We are going to bust them and bring them to their knees. Hopefully they will lead us east, to Chicago."

"We will be able to figure out when robberies and counterfeiting are taking place and how they are doing it. We will be one step ahead of them in every move they make," smiled Durango. "If we are going to beat these thugs we have to do it from the inside."

"We will have to be very smart about any information that we give them," says Diago. "Communication, our code words, their code words, anything you can get on them. Information is what we need to defeat them. Eddie it is up to you," concludes Diago. "This will be the toughest assign-ment you have had have so far."

"And remember," he adds, "When you are ready for Durango, we'll send him in. No need to rush, we'll send him in when you have established yourself and built up a good trust, so we can get Durango in without a problem. Once you have got

Durango in, we'll be able to work more efficiently getting information of what they are up to."

"But it will be up to you how you get inside the mob. That is why I picked you for the job Eddie: you are street smart and you got to have something of doing that will open the doors for you. Maybe have some background of working with others that they respect from another mob we have spies in that can vouch for you? Some mob that was run out of business by somebody else? But someone that has creditability," smirks Diago, "to get you in to this mob."

"Once we have got enough on them we'll bust them, sure as hell. Let's do this as fast as you can and as discreetly as possible. They won't even know what hit them if we do it right." Durango says. "Go get them Eddie. Report back to me at our favorite brothel and all will be smooth. Get me in there as fast as you can without being suspected."

• • •

A month went by, and then another month went by. Eddie was in the mob in a very good position. He was in charge of calculating plans for robberies. The police just let them go at the robbery without too much hassle, knowing it was a set-up.

The information started flowing in about the mob and finding out in depth who was in their pocket in the courts, and who all were on the take. All kinds of information was being found out, and Diago was always ready with the paperwork and other information to bust people and bring them down when the raids happen. Enough to keep control, but not enough that they get suspicious.

• • •

After meeting with Eddie, Durango reported, "Another month and we will have enough information to bring the mob to their knees."

"All the illegal betting, extortion, pay-offs, counterfeiting, and robberies will all be gone, all on one day," Diago said hungrily. "Their time was running short and it looks like the mob will be going down. That is what I like to hear."

"Next week we will have enough information to bring the high ranking members down," says Durango.

"They are other mobs in the city but we will be busting the biggest one in the territory," says Diago. "The others will fall."

• • •

"Have we got the SWAT briefed on how it is going down?" Durango asked.

"I am on it, Durango, no worries there," said Diago.

"Good because we worked hard for this and put our lives deeply on the line for this."

"Just the pay-offs of the public servants alone is

going to shake this city. Gamblers, robbers, extortionists, and counterfeiters will see their day when it hits."

"There will be enough fire power right, Diago?"

"We won't need much, they won't be expecting this to happen to them, now will, they?"

"Early morning is when we will strike while they are having a big conference in a room that day."

"That will make it easier for us to catch all of them in one room all at once, won't it?"

The day had come. It was early morning as planned and Diago charged into the room with the SWAT team and got them just when they were discussing how to rip off the town even more. Durango and Eddie didn't want to blow their cover, so they reluctantly stayed behind for the bust.

It was a well-planned bust—nobody fired a shot. They couldn't believe what was going on. The sorry looks on their faces told how surprised they were. Thirty powerful people of the community. And Durango and Eddie had good guys to take over their positions.

The district attorney was out for blood, to see that the mobsters got what they deserved. He was an arrogant man, but he did his job well. The criminals were going down to Yuma prison to do their time. That is where they all stayed while they were going to court for their crimes. Never before had such a big bust of the mob ever taken place without a shot. It was a sight to see.

Looking over the criminals in Yuma prison

awaiting their trial, Durango remarked, "Well, Eddie, it was good working with you again like this. Kind of like working for the Texas Rangers. The way we had to put our lives on the line working with them."

"Taming the town of Yuma wasn't an easy task either," Eddie reminded him.

"What is our next adventure?" Durango asked.

Epilogue

The town of Yuma has grown, and has a new sheriff by the name of Jericho. He has two deputies and their names are Mensa and Bronson. Together they make a wonderful team of lawmen. The town has grown.

It is still the 1800's. There is 400 people that have settled in Yuma since the story began, up from only 150. The infrastructure in Yuma has grown exponentially. All of the settlers have their own homes and ranches to live in. It has become a very busy town.

Putting a western rowdy town to tame so no one else in Yuma was to blame. The town is in good hands with Jericho as sheriff in command.

Jericho, Mensa and Samuel became best of friends along with Gracie and Shania. The stagecoach, then the train, was bringing in new settlers to Yuma quite often.

Jericho finally married Tricia from the diner. Pretty and sexy was an understatement. "She is gorgeous to come home to," he mentioned one day.

"I'll bet," was Gracie's response.

"Tricia and Jericho will live a long life of love and romance," smiles Katie Joe as she tells Durango the news.

Eddie said, "Dixie and I were going to take at least a month off and travel and see the sights on a passenger train. Then we will go out camping where there is no people around and have us a ball being together. No one for miles around is where we will be found."

The End

ABOUT THE AUTHOR

Ever since Faron Hanes was a young boy he was intrigued with being a cowboy. He would watch all of the John Wayne movies that they put out—this was his kind of cowboy: a rough and tough cowboy who never took any crap from other cowboys and was always on the good side of the law.

Along with John Wayne, Clint Eastwood was a favorite cowboy, too. When in the *Good, Bad, and the Ugly* he would spit just before he killed the outlaws... Josie Wales, the infamous cowboy that had a heart and killed only in self-defense. It was the same with Matt Dillon. They were his heroes, through-out his life. Faron would wear clothes just like them, and tried to talk like them.

Around the age of seven, just a little boy, he received his first horse, Blazer. He loved to ride this horse, and with his family he would take people on tours out on the trails. He groomed Blazer after every ride, and fed and cleaned up when he was in his stall. Even from this young age, he remembers how impressed his parents were with his discipline, and how responsible he was with Blazer.

Enjoying the company of his closest friends and

family who have always been impressed with the *country feel* of his stories, he eventually found the story of his life would be to write country songs and western books, telling tales of the old west.

Durango Outlaws is Faron's second book after *Gunslinger Durango* (to be re-released as *Durango West*). He is at work on a sequel, *Durango Rides Again* and a more personal memoir of his life.

HAPPY TRAILS